Little Red Riding Hood

Retold by **Bonnie Dobkin**

Illustrated by **Subhendu Karmakar**

TeachingStrategies® · Bethesda, MD

For Teaching Strategies, LLC.
Publisher: Larry Bram
Editorial Director: Hilary Parrish Nelson
VP Curriculum and Assessment: Cate Heroman
Product Manager: Kai-leé Berke
Book Development Team: Sherrie Rudick and Jan Greenberg
Project Manager: Jo A. Wilson

For Q2AMedia
Editorial Director: Bonnie Dobkin
Editor and Curriculum Adviser: Suzanne Barchers
Program Manager: Gayatri Singh
Creative Director: Simmi Sikka
Project Manager: Santosh Vasudevan
Illustrator: Subhendu Karmakar
Designers: Neha Kaul & Ritu Chopra

Teaching Strategies, LLC.
Bethesda, MD
www.TeachingStrategies.com

ISBN: 978-1-60617-132-5

Library of Congress Cataloging-in-Publication Data
Dobkin, Bonnie.
  Little Red Riding Hood / retold by Bonnie Dobkin ; illustrated by Subhendu Karmakar.
     p. cm.
  Summary: A little girl meets a hungry wolf in the forest while on her way to visit her grandmother.
  ISBN 978-1-60617-132-5
  [1. Fairy tales. 2. Folklore.] I. Karmakar, Subhendu, ill. II. Little Red Riding Hood. English. III. Title.
  PZ8.D650Lit 2010
  398.2--dc22
  [E]

                              2009037229

CPSIA tracking label information:
RR Donnelley, Shenzhen, China
Date of Production: August 2016
Cohort: Batch 5

Printed and bound in China

7 8 9 10	17 16
Printing	Year Printed

Once upon a time, a little girl lived with her mother and brother in a small cottage by the edge of a forest.

Her favorite piece of clothing was a long red cape with a soft silky hood. She wore it so often that soon everyone called her Little Red Riding Hood.

One day, Little Red Riding Hood was bored and looking for something to do.

"You could sweep the floors," said her mother, who was busy painting the fence.

"No," said Little Red Riding Hood. "I don't think that's what I want to do."

"You could help clean the yard," said
her brother, who was busy chopping wood.

"No," said Little Red Riding Hood.
"I *know* that isn't what I want to do!"

"Then you could visit your grandmother," said her mother. "You're old enough to go by yourself. And you haven't seen her for weeks."

"That's *exactly* what I want to do!" said Little Red Riding Hood. "Grandmother lives on the other side of the woods! It will be an adventure!"

So Little Red Riding Hood's mother packed a basket
full of treats for the girl to take to her grandmother.
"Just remember," said her mother, "the woods can
be very dangerous. So . . .

When you leave, please go straight—
Straight to Grandma's and don't be late."

"She won't listen," said her brother.

"Yes, I will," said Little Red Riding Hood.

"Of course she will," said her mother.
"Oh, and dear . . .

Something else, before you go.
Only talk to those you know."

"She won't listen," said her brother.

"Yes, I will," said Little Red Riding Hood.

"Of course she will," said her mother.
"Oh! And one last thing, sweetheart . . .

From the path you shouldn't stray
Or you could get lost someday."

"She won't listen," said her brother.

"Yes, I will," said Little Red Riding Hood.

"Of course she will," said her mother.
"Good-bye, dear! Give your
grandmother a big hug for me!"

"Yes, Mother," said Little Red Riding Hood.
Then she headed out the door, down the path,
and into the forest.

There was so much to see in the woods! A sleeping owl! A giant mushroom! An amazing spider web! Then Little Red Riding Hood remembered what her mother had said:

When you leave, please go straight—
Straight to Grandma's and don't be late.

But, thought Red Riding Hood, Mother surely would want me to enjoy the forest!

So she stopped and looked around.

11

Just then, a dark shape stepped out from
behind one of the trees. It was a wolf,
and he was smiling a charming smile.

"Why hello, little girl," said the wolf.
"Isn't this a lovely day!"

Little Red Riding Hood remembered
what her mother had said:

Something else, before you go.
Only talk to those you know.

But, thought Red Riding Hood, he seems like
such a friendly wolf! Mother surely wouldn't
want me to be rude.

13

"Hello, Mr. Wolf," said Little Red Riding Hood. "Yes, it is a lovely day!"

"And you seem to be such a delicious, by which I mean delightful, child." The wolf's smile grew even bigger. "What might your name be?"

"Everyone calls me Little Red Riding Hood," said the girl.

"A splendid name," said the wolf. "And where might you be headed, Little Red—if I may call you that?"

"You may," said Little Red Riding Hood. "I'm bringing my grandmother this basket of treats. She lives just on the other side of the forest."

"How kind of you!" the wolf said. "In fact, wouldn't your grandmother like a lovely bouquet of wildflowers, as well? There are some just over that hill, down by the edge of the river."

Red Riding Hood remembered what her mother said:

From the path you shouldn't stray
Or you could get lost someday.

But, thought Red Riding Hood, Mother surely would want me to bring Grandmother some flowers.

"That's a wonderful idea, Mr. Wolf! I'll pick some right away!" And she scampered off into the woods.

"Good-bye, Little Red!" the wolf called after her. "I'm sure we'll meet again very soon." And then he whispered, "By which I mean—for lunch!"

The moment Red Riding Hood disappeared, the wolf dashed down the path toward the grandmother's cottage. He tapped lightly on the door.

"Grandmother," he said, in his best little-girl voice. "It's me! Little Red Riding Hood!"

"Little Red? Really? How wonderful!"

Grandmother flung open the door.

"Wait," she said. "You're not Red Riding Hood."

"Sadly, no," said the wolf. "By which I mean—
good-bye!" And he swallowed the grandmother
in one big gulp!

"And now," said the wolf, patting his stomach,
"I'll wait for dessert."

Some time later, Red Riding Hood came out of the woods. She was dirty and rumpled, and there were burrs in her hair.

"It was much harder to find the path again than I thought it would be!" she said.

She was surprised to find her grandmother's door wide open. She stepped inside.

"Grandmother, are you home?"

"Yes, dear," came a scratchy voice from the bedroom. "But I'm in bed. I'm afraid I have a nasty cold."

Red Riding Hood followed the voice into the bedroom.
The curtains were closed, and it was very dark.
Grandmother was wearing a floppy nightcap,
and the blankets were pulled up past her nose.

Red Riding Hood moved toward the bed.
Grandmother's eyes looked very odd.

"Why, Grandmother," she said.
"What big eyes you have!"

"The better to see you with, my dear.
Come closer so I can give you a hug."

Red Riding Hood took another step and saw
two odd triangles poking up under the nightcap.

"And Grandmother, what big ears you have!"

"The better to hear you with, my dear.
Can you come a bit closer still?"

Just then the blankets slipped from the grandmother's face, revealing two rows of very sharp teeth!

"B-but Grandmother," said Red Riding Hood. "What big teeth you have!"

"THE BETTER TO EAT YOU WITH!" roared the wolf, leaping out of the grandmother's bed.

Red Riding Hood screamed. She ran out of the bedroom, through the main room, and into the kitchen, slamming doors behind her. She clambered into a cabinet and yanked the door shut.

Oh, why didn't I listen to Mother? she thought.

If I hadn't stopped in the woods, I wouldn't have met the wolf.

If I hadn't talked to the wolf, I wouldn't have left the path.

If I hadn't left the path, I wouldn't have been late to Grandmother's.

Then none of this would have happened!

In the kitchen, she could hear the wolf calling to her.

"Where are you, Little Red?" he said. "There's no need to hide. By which I mean, I'm going to find you and eat you, no matter what!"

Just then, something crashed.

A voice yelled.

Dishes smashed!

The sounds got louder and louder and wilder and wilder.

And then everything was quiet.

Little Red Riding Hood peeked out from the cabinet. There stood her brother, his ax in one hand. He was helping Grandmother step out of the wolf.

"Thank you, dear," said Grandmother. "It was very dark in there."

The brother looked at Little Red Riding Hood. "I *knew* you wouldn't listen."

Little Red Riding Hood scrambled out of the cabinet and gave her brother a big, big hug.

"You were right," she said. "But I will from now on!"

Then Red Riding Hood, her brother, and
their grandmother all sat down together
to eat the treats from the basket.